nickelodeon

PAW PATROL

BREAK THE ICE!

adapted by Courtney Carbone

based on the teleplay
"Pups and a Whale of a Tale"
by Andrew Guerdat

illustrated by MJ Illustrations

Random House 🏠 New York

Everest and Jake were
on Cap'n Turbot's boat.
It was cold.
Ice was everywhere.

Dear Parents:

Congratulations! Your child is taking the first steps on an exciting journey. The destination? Independent reading!

STEP INTO READING® will help your child get there. The program offers five steps to reading success. Each step includes fun stories and colorful art or photographs. In addition to original fiction and books with favorite characters, there are Step into Reading Non-Fiction Readers, Phonics Readers and Boxed Sets, Sticker Readers, and Comic Readers—a complete literacy program with something to interest every child.

Learning to Read, Step by Step!

Ready to Read   Preschool–Kindergarten
• big type and easy words • rhyme and rhythm • picture clues
For children who know the alphabet and are eager to begin reading.

Reading with Help   Preschool–Grade 1
• basic vocabulary • short sentences • simple stories
For children who recognize familiar words and sound out new words with help.

Reading on Your Own   Grades 1–3
• engaging characters • easy-to-follow plots • popular topics
For children who are ready to read on their own.

Reading Paragraphs   Grades 2–3
• challenging vocabulary • short paragraphs • exciting stories
For newly independent readers who read simple sentences with confidence.

Ready for Chapters   Grades 2–4
• chapters • longer paragraphs • full-color art
For children who want to take the plunge into chapter books but still like colorful pictures.

STEP INTO READING® is designed to give every child a successful reading experience. The grade levels are only guides; children will progress through the steps at their own speed, developing confidence in their reading.

Remember, a lifetime love of reading starts with a single step!

For my pup, Meggan –C.C.

© 2017 Spin Master PAW Productions Inc. All rights reserved. Published in the United States by Random House Children's Books, a division of Penguin Random House LLC, 1745 Broadway, New York, NY 10019, and in Canada by Penguin Random House Canada Limited, Toronto. PAW Patrol and all related titles, logos, and characters are trademarks of Spin Master Ltd. Nickelodeon, Nick Jr., and all related titles and logos are trademarks of Viacom International Inc.

Step into Reading, Random House, and the Random House colophon are registered trademarks of Penguin Random House LLC.

Visit us on the Web!
StepIntoReading.com
randomhousekids.com

Educators and librarians, for a variety of teaching tools, visit us at
RHTeachersLibrarians.com

ISBN 978-1-5247-6400-5 (trade) — ISBN 978-1-5247-6401-2 (lib. bdg.)

Printed in the United States of America

10 9 8 7 6 5 4 3 2 1

They saw a
mommy whale.
Her baby was lost!

Everest and Jake

looked near and far.

In the distance, they saw
the baby whale.
She was stuck
in the ice!

Everest and Jake

rushed to help

the baby whale.

But they could not
do it alone.

Everest and Jake
knew they needed help.

They called Ryder.

Ryder and the
pups raced to
the Air Patroller.

The PAW Patrol flew
to the Ice Fields.
The pups were ready
to work!

First, Rubble drilled
holes in the ice.

Next, Rocky cut
out blocks
of ice with a saw.

Then Everest pulled

the blocks away

with a big hook.

Soon the pups had made
a path of holes back to
the sea!

But the baby whale
did not know
what to do.

Ryder had an idea.
The baby whale
could follow Everest
on her snowboard!

Everest jumped over
the holes one by one.
Jump! Jump! Jump!

The baby whale followed.

Splash! Splash! Splash!

The baby whale jumped
all the way back
to the mommy whale!

Hooray!
The PAW Patrol
saved the day!

Dear Parents:

Congratulations! Your child is taking the first steps on an exciting journey. The destination? Independent reading!

STEP INTO READING® will help your child get there. The program offers five steps to reading success. Each step includes fun stories and colorful art or photographs. In addition to original fiction and books with favorite characters, there are Step into Reading Non-Fiction Readers, Phonics Readers and Boxed Sets, Sticker Readers, and Comic Readers—a complete literacy program with something to interest every child.

Learning to Read, Step by Step!

Ready to Read   Preschool–Kindergarten
• big type and easy words • rhyme and rhythm • picture clues
For children who know the alphabet and are eager to begin reading.

Reading with Help   Preschool–Grade 1
• basic vocabulary • short sentences • simple stories
For children who recognize familiar words and sound out new words with help.

Reading on Your Own   Grades 1–3
• engaging characters • easy-to-follow plots • popular topics
For children who are ready to read on their own.

Reading Paragraphs   Grades 2–3
• challenging vocabulary • short paragraphs • exciting stories
For newly independent readers who read simple sentences with confidence.

Ready for Chapters   Grades 2–4
• chapters • longer paragraphs • full-color art
For children who want to take the plunge into chapter books but still like colorful pictures.

STEP INTO READING® is designed to give every child a successful reading experience. The grade levels are only guides; children will progress through the steps at their own speed, developing confidence in their reading.

Remember, a lifetime love of reading starts with a single step!

Step into Reading, Random House, and the Random House colophon are registered trademarks of Penguin Random House LLC.

Visit us on the Web!
StepIntoReading.com
randomhousekids.com

Educators and librarians, for a variety of teaching tools, visit us at
RHTeachersLibrarians.com

ISBN 978-1-5247-6400-5 (trade) — ISBN 978-1-5247-6401-2 (lib. bdg.)

Printed in the United States of America

10 9 8 7 6 5 4 3 2 1

EVEREST SAVES THE DAY!

adapted by Tex Huntley

based on the teleplay "The New Pup"
by Ursula Ziegler Sullivan

illustrated by MJ Illustrations

Random House 🏠 New York

The pups are going

on a trip.

They will ride in
the PAW Patroller.

Robo Dog will drive
the PAW Patroller.
All the pups
are excited.

Just then, Jake calls.

He can't wait

to see the pups.

They are going to visit
him at the Ice Fields.

Suddenly, Jake slips
on the ice.

His pack slides
into a river!

Jake is in trouble!
The pups roll
their trucks onto
the PAW Patroller.

It is time to race
to the Ice Fields.

Meanwhile, Jake
slides toward
the river.
A pup saves him!

The pup's name
is Everest.
She is a husky
and a hero!

Chase and Ryder
search the Ice Fields.
They find Jake's tracks.

At the same time,

Skye searches

from the air.

She sees something!

Jake and Everest

cross an ice bridge.

Crack! Crack!

Oh, no!
The ice bridge
is breaking!

Jake falls!

Everest grabs him!

Jake is safe.

Everest gets a badge.
Now she is part
of the PAW Patrol!

Hooray for Everest!

She is one cool pup!